"Aren't you interested in Sophie's party?"

"No," said Patrick.

"Why not?"

There was silence.

Then Luke spoke. "He doesn't like parties."

Tamsin gaped at Patrick as if he was a Being from Another Planet. "You don't like parties?"

"No."

"You can't not like parties!"

"I can."

"But . . . what's not to like?"

Patrick shrugged. "Everything." He felt he had to add something. "All the . . . fuss!"

"Oh, I love all the fuss!" Tamsin's eyes shone. "Fuss is what makes a party! The clothes, the food – everything! Parties are" – she wriggled her shoulders, trying to think of the right word – "special! Otherwise everything's the same all the time!"

Patrick said nothing. There was no point.

www.kidsatrandomhouse.co.uk

YOUNG CORGI BOOKS

Young Corgi books are perfect when you are looking for great books to read on your own. They are full of exciting stories and entertaining pictures. There are funny books, scary books, spine-tingling stories and mysterious ones. Whatever your interests you'll find something in Young Corgi to suit you, from ponies to football, from families and friends to ghosts. The books are written by some of the most famous and popular of today's children's authors, and by some of the best new talents, too.

Whether you read one chapter a night, or devour the whole book in one sitting, you'll love Young Corgi Books. The more you read, the more you'll want to read!

Other Young Corgi Books to get your teeth into:
THE PROMPTER by Chris D'Lacey
ZEUS ON THE LOOSE by John Dougherty
BILLY AND THE SEAGULLS by Paul May
SPUD by Alison Prince

Patrick the Party-Hater

Emily Smith

Illustrated by Georgie Birkett

PATRICK THE PARTY-HATER
A YOUNG CORGI BOOK : 0 552 55173 2

Published in Great Britain by Corgi Books,
an imprint of Random House Children's Books

This edition published 2004

3 5 7 9 10 8 6 4 2

Papers used by Random House Children's Books are natural, recyclable products made from wood grown in sustainable forests. The manufuacturing processes conform to the environmental regulations of the country of origin.

Set in 17/21pt Bembo Schoolbook by
Falcon Oast Graphic Art Ltd.

Corgi Books are published by Random House Children's Books,
61–63 Uxbridge Road, London W5 5SA,
a division of The Random House Group Ltd,
in Australia by Random House Australia (Pty) Ltd,
20 Alfred Street, Milsons Point, Sydney, NSW 2061, Australia,
in New Zealand by Random House New Zealand Ltd,
18 Poland Road, Glenfield, Auckland 10, New Zealand
and in South Africa by Random House (Pty) Ltd,
Endulini, 5a Jubilee Road, Parktown 2193, South Africa

THE RANDOM HOUSE GROUP Limited Reg. No. 954009
www.**kidsatrandomhouse**.co.uk

A CIP catalogue record for this book is available from the British Library.

Printed and bound in Great Britain by
Cox & Wyman Ltd, Reading, Berkshire.

For Michael, who loves parties

One

It was scary.

Patrick was in the middle of a ring of children.

They were holding hands and singing something.

It was really scary.

He was stuck in the middle – no doubt about that. And they knew he was stuck too.

They were smiling and laughing. They were enjoying themselves.

But he wasn't.

Not one bit.

Which was odd.

Because he was at a party.

He was supposed to be enjoying himself. Wasn't he?

Patrick was older now. Years older.

He had only been a little kid when he went to that party – but he still remembered it.

And he didn't like parties.

He hated them.

He hated everything about them.

So he knew there was trouble ahead when Sophie started handing out envelopes in the playground.

Pink envelopes.

Pink envelopes with balloons on.

Patrick reckoned that pink envelopes with balloons could mean only one thing. Aaaargh!

"She's got a lot there," said Patrick's friend Luke.

Patrick nodded.

"Maybe she's asked the whole class," said Luke.

"I hope so," said Tamsin Rees, who was standing nearby. "It's not *kind* to give out invitations in school if you haven't asked the whole class."

"It saves on stamps," said Luke.

"*Stamps!*" Tamsin snorted. "I'm talking about *kindness*!"

Luke shrugged.

"Look!" cried Tamsin. "She's giving one to Hannah. I haven't talked to Hannah for ages!" And she was gone.

"I've got some ball bearings at home," said Patrick.

"What are ball bearings?" said Luke.

Patrick started explaining about ball bearings. "Well, they're silver balls, and they—"

Suddenly Sophie was racing up to them. She held something in her hand. A pink envelope. "Luke!" she called out.

Luke held out his hand. Sophie gave

him the envelope. Patrick watched him take it.

OK, Luke had one.

But that didn't mean that *he* was invited, did it?

Could Sophie really ask *everyone* in their class. All thirty-two of them?

But Sophie was still standing in front of them. She was leafing through a still-quite-thick pile of envelopes. "Charlie . . . Kevin . . . Patrick!" She held out a pink envelope towards Patrick.

He read the name on the cover. *Patric*. "Not me!" he said brightly.

Sophie frowned, and looked at the envelope again. "It is!"

"No! I've got a K at the end of my name!"

"Of course it's you!" said Sophie.

"That's not how I spell my name!" said Patrick.

"Well, it's you in my head!" insisted Sophie. And she thrust it into his hand and ran off.

Luke had opened his envelope, and was now studying a pink card. "It's my birthday . . . It's my birthday . . ." He put his head on one side. "It's my birthday." He turned the card round slowly. "Come and . . . join the . . . fun."

Patrick stuffed his envelope into his trouser pocket, unopened. He was still thinking of the best way to explain ball bearings.

Tamsin bounced up again, waving her invitation. "She *has* asked everyone in our class! It's at her house! And they've got a conjuror coming!"

Patrick turned to Luke. "They're metal balls," he said. "And they make things—"

"*What* are you talking about?" said Tamsin.

"Ball bearings," said Patrick.

"*Ball bearings?* Aren't you interested in Sophie's party?"

"No," said Patrick.

"Why not?"

There was silence.

Then Luke spoke. "He doesn't like parties."

Tamsin gaped at Patrick as if he was a Being from Another Planet. "You don't like parties?"

"No."

"You can't not like parties!"

"I can."

"But . . . what's not to like?"

Patrick shrugged. "Everything." He felt he had to add something. "All the . . . fuss!"

"Oh, I love all the fuss!" Tamsin's eyes shone. "Fuss is what makes a party! The clothes, the food – everything! Parties are" – she wriggled her shoulders, trying to

think of the right word – "special! Otherwise everything's the same all the time!"

Patrick said nothing. There was no point.

"So you won't be coming, then?" Tamsin tucked her invitation back into its envelope.

"Um . . . I might be," said Patrick.

Tamsin raised her eyebrows. "You might be?"

"His mum makes him," Luke explained.

"Hey, tough call!" said Tamsin.

"Yes," said Patrick. "It is rather tough."

Tamsin frowned. "But *why* does your mum make you?"

Patrick thought. "I don't know, really. She just does."

Tamsin looked at him kindly. She was obviously trying to think of something nice to say.

Then she thought of something nice to say.

Well, she thought it was nice.

But it wasn't.

It was stupid.

"Oh, well! I expect you'll enjoy it when you get there!"

Two

Patrick was watching television.

It was a programme he liked *bits* of. There were too many interviews with boy bands. And not enough bits where they showed you how to make things.

Patrick liked making things. He

had made a Delta Wing Jet after a programme once.

Ah! There was Debbi, the blonde presenter, at a table. This looked promising.

Debbi was smiling. "Have *I* got something for you to make!" she said.

Well, had she?

The camera zoomed in on . . . what? It was a strange construction with turrets and slopes and girders.

Debbi held up a marble, and smiled again. "Does this give you a clue?"

It did give Patrick a clue.

He guessed at once.

A marble run . . .

Patrick had never made a marble run before. He had never even thought about making a marble run before . . .

"*Patrick! I found something in your trousers!*"

Debbi was now holding up some cereal boxes and stuff. "These are all you need to make your marble run—"

"*Patrick! I nearly put it in the wash!*"

Debbi was assembling the run now. "Cereal boxes form the base – as so. And then you stick these long boxes and sweet tubes on the top and sides. But first you must get your scissors and—"

"*Patrick! A lovely invitation from Sophie Grant!*"

Patrick turned. His mother was standing in the doorway, holding the pink card. Her eyes glowed. "How kind of her to ask you!"

"She's asked everyone in the whole class," said Patrick.

"Oh, what fun! How nice of them. Such a nice family, the Grants. You went there in the summer when I had

to work late, you remember?"

"I remember."

"I rang Mrs Grant in a total panic, and she couldn't have been nicer!" Mum recalled happily. "They're such an interesting family, too. The father's a writer, you know. History . . . or politics – or something!"

Patrick looked back at the

television. Debbi was painting the marble run now. She was painting it red. Patrick thought that if he made a marble run, he would probably paint it blue and white. Or maybe – if he used his ball bearings – blue and silver.

"We must think what present to take!" said Mum. "Now, what do girls like . . . ?"

"Mum," said Patrick.

"What?"

"I don't want to go," said Patrick.

"Oh, not this nonsense again!" cried Mum. "Of course you must go!"

"I don't want to."

"Look, Patrick!" Mum came and sat next to him on the sofa. "Going to parties – joining in – is important."

Patrick said nothing.

"You're very lucky to be asked."

Patrick said nothing.

"I'd have *loved* that sort of party when I was your age."

Patrick said nothing.

She tried to meet his eye, but he avoided her gaze.

"Oh, Patrick!" Mum flapped the pink card in the air. "You can't *not* do things just because you think you won't enjoy them!"

Couldn't he? It seemed very reasonable to him.

"Maybe you have to *learn* to enjoy parties." Mum got to her feet. "But you will!" She put the pink card on the mantelpiece, turned and smiled at him. "Believe me – you will!"

She went out.

Patrick looked back at the television screen.

Debbi had got a bit of red paint on the tip of her nose . . .

Three

"*Hullo?*" Luke barked down the phone.

"Is this a good moment?" said Patrick.

"Yes," said Luke. "I'm waiting for my Gnome King to dry."

"Ah," said Patrick. "Well, I want you to collect toothpaste boxes."

"Toothpaste boxes? What are toothpaste boxes?"

"They're the boxes that tubes of toothpaste come in," explained Patrick. "You can collect Smarties tubes too, but I don't think they're so good."

"Patrick."

"What?"

"I'm not interested in toothpaste boxes. I collect war game models – you know I do. I've nearly completed my Gnome Cohort now. And my Undeads are building nicely."

Patrick sighed. Luke did collect fantasy war game models. Patrick tried to take an interest in Luke's models, but sometimes it was hard.

"Look, Luke. I'm not talking about *collecting* toothpaste boxes. Just . . . collecting them."

Rather to Patrick's surprise, Luke understood this. "Oh. So what are these toothpaste boxes for?"

"I'm going to build a marble run."

"Patrick."

"Yes?"

"You can buy marble runs."

"Not like mine, you can't. Mine is going to be *enormous*. I'm calling it Marble Run City. That's why I need as many toothpaste boxes as possible. Or Smarties tubes. But I don't think they're so good."

Luke said, "OK."

"You will?"

"Yes. I'll raid the bathroom. Then the sisters' bedrooms. Then I'll eat any Smarties I can get my hands on. Then I'll clean my teeth."

"Right!"

"And I won't even wait for my Gnome King to dry . . ."

"I bought you some new stuff," said Mum, coming into his room.

"Thanks, Mum," Patrick said.

"Yes." Mum opened a plastic bag. "You need something new to wear for the party."

"*What?*"

"New clothes. For the party. You've grown out of all your smart stuff."

Patrick gazed at Mum. "I don't need smart clothes."

"To go to a party at the Grants'?" Mum gave him a look. "I think so." She pulled out some navy trousers and a cream shirt with buttons on the collar. "You'll look cool in these!"

Cool? *Cool?* The woman didn't know the meaning of the word!

Patrick stared at the clothes.

Oh, well, next Saturday was still some time off.

Maybe a meteorite would hit Earth before then, and wipe out all life forms.

Then he wouldn't have to go to Sophie's party . . .

Four

The faces circled round him. They were grinning. And singing.

It was Saturday.

Patrick woke with a feeling that something terrible was going to happen.

And then he realized that something terrible *was* going to happen.

Sophie's party.

He had got the Party Feeling in his stomach. He burrowed his head down under his duvet.

Oh, why hadn't he chucked the invitation in a bin!

Or torn it into a thousand pink pieces?

Even a small fire would have done the trick.

Why had he just left it in his trousers?

There was no help for it. He would have to go to the party. Unless . . . unless . . .

Patrick frowned and lifted his head out of his duvet. It had never worked before. But maybe – just maybe – it would work this time. "Mum!" he called weakly. "Mum!"

No answer.

"Mum!" he shouted a bit louder.

She stuck her head round the door.

"What?"

Patrick looked at her and screwed up his face. "I feel ill!"

"Ill where?"

"Ill all over!"

Mum felt his forehead, and then went to get the thermometer.

"Normal!" she said brightly when she took it out of his mouth. "You're fine!"

But he wasn't fine at all. He had the Party Feeling . . .

Funnily enough, he managed to forget the party for most of the morning.

He tried out designs for Marble Run City.

He had gathered quite a lot of suitable building material now. His

Uncle Duncan, who was a keen cook, had given him lots of boxes from stuff Patrick had never even heard of, like anchovy paste. Uncle Duncan had also had the brilliant idea of using silver foil boxes (now why hadn't Debbi thought of that?).

Mum grumbled that his room was even more of a tip than usual, but she hadn't got seriously cross.

Height was the thing, he decided, as he knelt on the floor, surrounded by boxes.

Marble Run City was going to be higher than Debbi's marble run.

Marble Run City was going to be faster than Debbi's marble run.

Marble Run City was going to be way more exciting than Debbi's marble run.

Yup. It was going to *soar*.

The big cardboard box first, then the big cereal boxes on top of that, then the smaller cereal boxes on *them*, then—

"Time to get ready!" called Mum suddenly.

His hand slipped sideways.

Boxes cascaded to the floor.

Patrick rose slowly to his feet . . .

A few minutes later, he was staring at himself in his mirror.

What were the buttons on his shirt collar for?

"Rhona just rang," said Mum, coming in.

When would you ever want to unbutton a shirt collar?

"She was trying to ring all morning, apparently."

Could you button the buttons onto the wrong buttonholes without strangling yourself?

"Luke won't be going to the party."

Suddenly Patrick registered what she was saying. "*What?*"

Mum sighed. "We were going to share the run, too."

"Luke not going to the party?"

"No."

"But why?"

"He's ill," said Mum.

"Luke's not ill! Luke can't be ill! Luke's never ill!"

Mum looked at him. "Temperature of a hundred and one. Shivering all over. Luke's ill all right."

"You know what?" said Mum, as she drove Patrick along. "Your own birthday's not far off now."

"Mmmm." Patrick was watching a distant crane as it swung through the air.

"So we ought to start thinking about parties."

"I don't want to think about parties."

Slowly, smoothly, the crane moved its load round. Patrick imagined the operator high up in his cabin, at the controls. All alone, and all-powerful.

"Well, not parties exactly. What I mean is, *your* party."

"My party?" Now he was staring at the back of Mum's head in horror.

"Yes. Your party! It's lucky your birthday falls on a Saturday this year. There's not enough room at the flat, of course. So I thought we might take the church h—"

"But I don't want a party!"

Mum laughed. "Oh, Patrick!"

"Look, Mum! It's bad enough going to other people's—"

"Sssh! I've got to concentrate on finding the way. I'm sure I remember passing this shop."

"Mum!"

"There's the turn!" Mum slammed

on the brakes, then swung the car to the right, up a side road. Then she took a left. "Now, it should be about halfway up here—"

"Mum! Please! I don't want a party!"

"Later!" Mum drove him jerkily up the tree-lined road, stopping to peer at house numbers. "You just enjoy Sophie's party first. We'll talk about your party later!"

Five

A silver gas balloon was tied to Sophie's gate. Patrick watched it bobbing gently in the air. Somehow the balloon meant the party was for real.

It was the right day.

It was the right house.

It was the right time.

There was going to be a party.

And he, Patrick, was going to it.

The Party Feeling in his stomach had grown.

Patrick was just about to give the silver balloon a good punch, when he heard a shout.

He turned to see a strange figure racing towards him.

It was pink.

Pink and floaty.

A pink and floaty figure he didn't think he had ever seen before.

But then it got closer. And he realized he had seen it before. It was Tamsin.

"Hi! Patrick!" Tamsin skidded to a stop in front of him, laughing in delight. "This is my bridesmaid's dress! Do you think it's a bit over the top?" She twirled round in a froth of pink. Then she stopped and looked at his face. "Are you OK?"

Patrick said nothing.

"You're *not* OK." Tamsin looked around. "Where's Luke?"

Patrick sighed. "He's ill."

"Oh. Rats!"

"Yeah," said Patrick. "Rats."

Tamsin smiled at him. "Well, then!"

"What do you mean, well then?" said Patrick.

Tamsin nodded towards the front door. "You come in with me!"

They went through the gate and started up the pathway.

The two mums followed them.

"She loves dressing up!" Patrick heard Tamsin's mum say.

"*Does she?*" said Mum.

"Been ready for hours!"

"*Has she?*" said Mum.

"She's a real party-girl!"

"*Is she?*" said Mum.

And Patrick thought he heard Mum give a little sigh . . .

Before they had reached the door, it was flung open. There, on the threshold, stood a beaming Sophie.

"Tamsin! Patrick!" she cried. "Oh, and Kevin and Charlie!"

Patrick turned. Yes. Kevin and Charlie were a few steps behind them. And just turning into the gate was a tall girl Patrick had never seen before.

Everyone crowded into the hall. Tamsin grabbed a big rainbow-coloured present from her mum, and tumbled it into Sophie's arms. "Hope you like it! If not, can I have it back?"

"*Tamsin!*" hissed her mum.

The rainbow present was followed by two smaller ones from Kevin and Charlie, and a card from the tall girl.

"Presents!" said Mrs Grant briskly, stepping forward. "How lovely! But don't open them now, Sophie! You'll get into a muddle and forget who gave you what! Put them . . . put them in Daddy's study!"

"OK, Mum!" Sophie opened a door off the hall – and dashed through it.

In a few seconds she was out again, without the presents.

But she was not alone.

Six

Sophie came dashing out of "Daddy's study".

And then someone came out after her.

It had to be "Daddy". Or rather, Mr Grant. And a very surprised Mr Grant at that.

He peered at the crowd in his hall in complete amazement. "What the—?" He clapped a hand to his head. "The *party*!"

"Yes, Daddy!" cried Sophie. "My party! Don't say you'd forgotten!"

"No!" said Mr Grant quickly. "Of course not!"

"It's my biggest party ever!" Sophie's face was shining. "Twenty-four friends from school, and five friends not from school! We're going

to play crazy disco games off a CD! And Sardines right through house!"

Mr Grant drew a deep breath.

Then he looked at his watch.

Then he said, "Is that really the time? I must get a move on."

"What do you mean, you must get a move on?" cried Sophie. "Aren't you staying for my party?"

Mr Grant looked at his daughter. "I can't," he said sadly. "I . . . I have to get to the library before it closes." He glanced round at the mums. "Deadlines," he murmured. "Always the deadlines . . ."

"But you'll miss Uncle Dickie!" said Sophie.

"Uncle Dickie?" Mr Grant looked uncertain. "Would that be one of your mother's relations?"

"*No*, Daddy!" said Sophie. "Uncle Dickie's the conjuror!"

"Ah, the conjuror. The conjuror." Mr Grant eyed the front door. "Well, maybe I'll be back in time for the conjuror."

"He's straight after tea!" said Sophie.

Mr Grant looked down at his daughter and touched her lightly on the cheek. "Have fun, sweetheart," he said softly. Then he plunged through the crowd, and was out of the door.

Patrick watched Mr Grant walk briskly down the garden path, walk briskly through the gate (making the balloon wobble violently) and walk briskly away up the road.

And Patrick's heart sang.

For he *knew*.

That stuff about the library hadn't fooled him for one moment. (And what a bad liar Mr Grant was. Patrick himself wasn't a good liar, but he was much better than Mr Grant!)

Patrick's heart sang because he knew he had come across . . . another one. Another party-hater!

Everyone had always thought Patrick so odd for not liking parties.

Mum, Tamsin, Sophie – no one could understand it at all. Even his friend Luke didn't really get it. It made Patrick feel different and . . . alone.

But now he knew he wasn't alone after all.

It didn't matter that Mr Grant was much older than him.

It didn't matter that Mr Grant had never even spoken to him.

All that mattered was Mr Grant was . . . a fellow party-hater!

Seven

Everyone poured into the front room.

"Right, guys!" Mrs Grant shouted. "Are you too old for Musical Bumps?"

"Yes!" shouted half the guests.

"No!" shouted the other half.

"We'll play it then," she said, to a mixture of cheers and boos. "At least everyone knows it."

"I don't know it!" said Kevin.

"Nor me!" said Charlie.

Mrs Grant gave them a look. "Well, just try to pick it up as you go along . . ."

So the games started.

Musical Bumps was not a problem for Patrick.

"Don't bump!" was the answer to

that one. Then you get to sit out. And think about something interesting, like marble runs . . .

And, funnily enough, he did this quite happily. He didn't feel he *ought* to be enjoying himself. Mr Grant had shown him that.

But Tamsin played to win. The pink floaty dress didn't stop her dropping like a stone whenever the music stopped. She got into the very last round, but then lost to the tall girl.

After Musical Bumps came Hot Chocolate. You had to throw dice until you got a six, and then you put on funny clothes, and ate a bar of chocolate with a knife and fork.

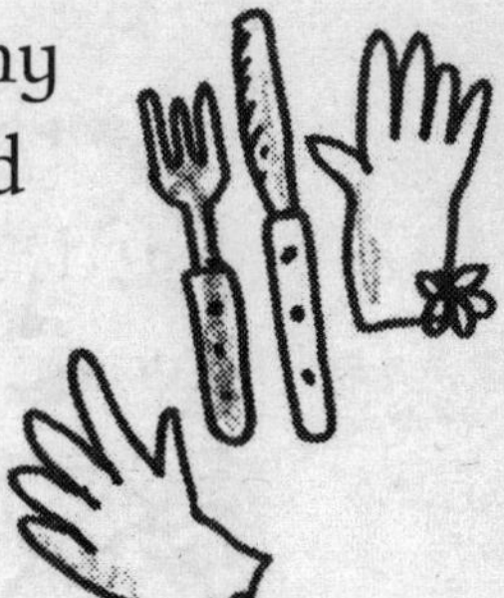

Patrick watched Charlie cheating. This was interesting but not surprising.

He watched Mrs Grant watching Charlie cheating, and not doing anything about it. This was interesting, and perhaps more surprising.

After Hot Chocolate came the "crazy disco party games".

It got noisier and noisier. Kevin tripped over Charlie, and suddenly they were both punching each other. Mrs Grant pulled them apart.

Patrick watched her yelling at them, pink in the face. He thought of the time he had come round for tea in the summer. They had talked about dinosaurs (it had been his dinosaur phase), and Mrs Grant had been really interesting. She knew more about triceratops than any mother he had ever met.

Yes, that was one of the troubles with parties. They made people so different . . .

Suddenly Mrs Grant was clapping her hands. "Tea, everyone!" she said. "Tea time!" And everyone started trooping into the kitchen.

Patrick was just thinking it might be nice to have the front room to himself for a bit, when Tamsin grabbed him by hand. "Come on!" she said in an undertone. "Let's get a good space!"

They were all given a cardboard picnic box, and told to find a space on the kitchen floor. Tamsin and Patrick sat by the kitchen table. Whether this was a "good space" or not, Patrick wasn't sure. But he opened his picnic box happily enough.

Peanut butter sandwich . . . Marmite sandwich . . . plain crisps . . . carrot sticks . . . little bunch of grapes . . . chocolate crispie thing . . . box of apple juice. Good . . .. OK . . . could be better . . . OK-ish . . . OK . . . good . . . good.

After eating some of his tea, Patrick started playing with the straw in his box of apple juice.

He liked straws. He had liked straws ever since he was little.

Sucking was good. Blowing was good. Sucking juice up the straw and holding it there with his finger was good too.

As he held the straw above his head and let the juice whoosh into his mouth, he heard Tamsin say, "Uh-oh."

He followed her gaze to see Mrs Grant standing at the open oven with some oven gloves. Sophie was beside her. They were both staring into the oven in dismay.

"They're still pink!" said Sophie.

"And stone cold!" Mrs Grant put her hand down. "But how—?"

"We must have sausages!" wailed Sophie. "I've got all the sticks in a pot!"

Mrs Grant shook her head. "We can't. They're not done."

"But you must have sausages at a party!" said Sophie.

Someone else had heard.

"Sausages!" chanted Kevin. "Soss, soss – sausages!"

So had someone else.

"We're waiting for our sausages!" shouted Charlie.

"Soss, soss – sausages!"

"We want sausages!"

"Soss, soss—"

Mrs Grant flung the oven gloves on top of the grill and turned on them. "Be quiet, the pair of you!"

Charlie and Kevin looked at each

other and grinned . . .

The cake came quickly after that. It was a gingerbread house. Tamsin said a polite "no thank you" to some wall and managed to get two slices of roof (which was made of chocolate buttons).

She was good at that sort of thing, Patrick thought, munching gratefully.

A little cheer went up as the first people went back to the front room.

Sophie looked at her mother. "Is that Uncle Dickie?"

Mrs Grant looked at her watch. "Must be."

With a flurry of pink, Tamsin was gone. Other people raced after her. Soon Patrick was the only person left in the kitchen.

He turned back to his straw. His apple juice was finished, but there was still Tamsin's half-empty glass of fizzy orange. (Somehow Tamsin had managed to get fizzy orange after finishing her apple juice.) He looked at the bubbles fizzing. Did bubbles go up the straw? Even a thin straw like this one? Surely they did? Or did they?

Well, there was one way to find out. He picked the glass up, dropped the straw in and put the end of the straw carefully in his mouth . . .

"Oh!" said a voice.

Patrick jumped.

He turned to see Mrs Grant standing at the door.

Mrs Grant gave a no-nonsense smile.

Mrs Grant pointed a no-nonsense finger towards the front room.

Mrs Grant said, in a no-nonsense tone, "Conjuror time!"

Eight

Patrick crept into the front room and found a place on the floor at the back of the crowd.

He peered between Kevin and Charlie's heads to see a man in a funny suit pulling handkerchiefs from thin air.

Uncle Dickie.

Uncle Dickie had a smile on his face.

It was a pleased-with-himself sort of smile.

It was, well, more of a smirk, really.

Uncle Dickie seemed to smirk a lot.

A trick with wooden hoops came next. Then Uncle Dickie turned to his audience. "Now, would any boy or girl like to help with my next—"

Tamsin was on her feet before he could say "trick".

He smiled down at her. "And what's your name, dear?"

"Tamsin!" said Tamsin, grinning.

"Really?" Uncle Dickie gave a wink. "Why, that was my name when I was a little girl."

Tamsin giggled.

The audience tittered.

The smirk deepened.

Patrick's gaze wandered round the room.

And stopped at the half-open door.

He stared thoughtfully at the door.

The door led to the passage.

The passage led to the garden door.

The garden door led to . . . the garden.

Patrick thought about the time he had come round to Sophie's in the summer. It had been a lovely day, and they had raced straight from car to garden. *Yes.* There had been a trampoline . . . and a climbing frame . . . and a sandpit.

Some people grow out of sandpits.

Other people do not grow out of sandpits.

Patrick was one of the people who

do not grow out of sandpits.

And the Grants' sandpit wasn't just any old sandpit.

It was big, for a start.

It had lots of sand in it too.

But, best of all, it had a digger in it. A real digger (well, as real a digger as you could get in a sandpit).

The digger was metal. You sat on it and used two sets of levers to work a scoop to pick up sand and move it around.

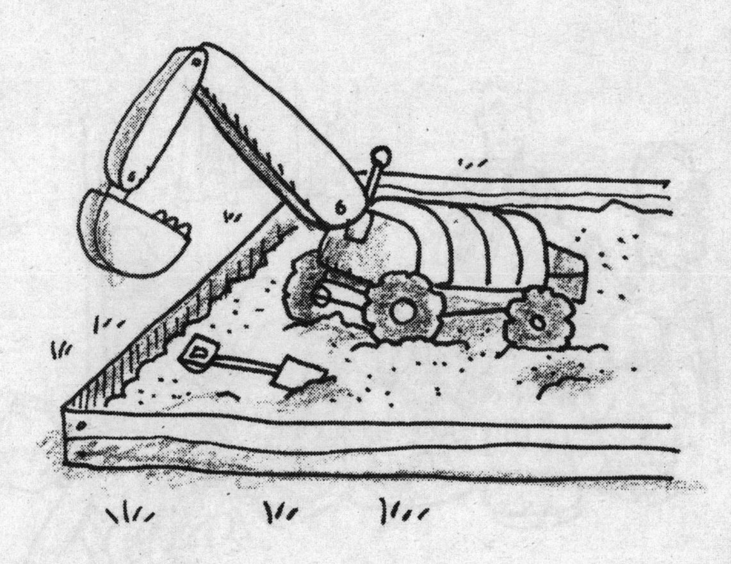

It was great. Actually, it was better than great. It was ace. Patrick drew a deep breath.

Everyone's eyes were fixed on Uncle Dickie. There was laughter as he handed Tamsin a magic wand, and it promptly collapsed.

Slowly Patrick starting crawling past people's backs.

He glimpsed Mrs Grant smiling at the side, holding up a camera.

He crawled on.

He heard Tamsin being given another wand.

He crawled on.

In the corner of his eye he saw Uncle Dickie holding out a big golden box.

He crawled on.

Now Patrick was nearly to the door.

"Tap it three times with your wand!" he heard Uncle Dickie say to Tamsin. "One!"

Patrick was out of the room.

"Two!"

Patrick was down the passage, turning the handle of the garden door.

"Three!" he heard very faintly.

But he was out in the chilly autumn garden.

Abracadabra!

Nine

Patrick looked around the leaf-strewn garden.

It seemed very different to that day in the summer. The trampoline was gone, but the climbing frame was still there – and so was the sandpit.

Patrick ran over and grabbed the heavy wooden lid by its handle. He heaved it three-quarters of the way off – then peered down. No! Disappointment flooded through him. Dampish sand, a small spade and a few faded plastic toys – that was all. No digger to be seen.

Suddenly he wanted to see that digger. He had a picture of it in his head in all its glorious yellow.

Where was it?

Patrick looked around. He

remembered a big garden shed at the bottom of the garden. It had been half hidden by bushes in the summer. Now it stood there, quite obvious. It seemed just the sort of place you would store a digger . . .

Patrick started walking down the garden.

The shed had two greenish windows, which were slightly open – and a door, which was shut. Patrick stepped up to it, put his hand to the latch – and pulled.

The door *was* shut.

But it *wasn't* locked.

It swung back silently in his hand.

Patrick took a step inside and, as he did so, he heard a noise.

A noise of something moving.

There was something – or someone – in the shed!

Patrick froze, his mind racing. What was it?

A rat? A puma? An axe murderer?

His heart was hammering now. The garden shed felt a long way from the house. A *very* long way from the house.

Then there was a cough. And suddenly his eyes became accustomed to the gloom – and he saw what it was.

It wasn't a rat.

It wasn't a puma.

It wasn't an axe murderer.

It was Mr Grant.

Ten

Mr Grant was sitting in a chair in front of a workbench, with an open book in his hands.

He was looking at Patrick.

The look in his eyes wasn't angry. It wasn't even surprised. It was more . . . guilty.

"Have you come to get me?" said Mr Grant.

"No," said Patrick.

"Do they know I'm here?"

"No," said Patrick.

"Do you think I should go back?"

"No," said Patrick. "Not if you don't want to."

There was silence.

Patrick looked beyond Mr Grant to the workbench. It was a proper wooden workbench, with clamps and saws hanging up to one side, and a

vice fixed to the front. Patrick gazed at the vice. It looked shiny, fairly new. He would really like to have a go with that vice . . .

Suddenly he was aware that Mr Grant was speaking. ". . . very good to see you. But may I ask what are you doing here? Shouldn't you be at . . . er . . . the party?"

The question hung in the air.

Then Patrick said, "I don't like parties much."

Mr Grant said, "No, I don't like parties much either."

Their eyes met.

Then Patrick nodded towards the workbench. "But I like making things. I'm making a marble run at the moment."

"Really?" Mr Grant looked at him. "Is that why you came out to the shed?"

"No," said Patrick. "I didn't know there was a workbench here. I was looking for the digger."

"The digger?"

"Yes. The digger that used to be in the sandpit."

"Oh, the *digger*!" cried Mr Grant. "Well, I can tell you what happened to that! It's bust."

"Bust?"

"Bust." Mr Grant's face darkened. "Only the other day – by some of my wife's relations."

"Oh," said Patrick.

There was a pause.

"And it couldn't be mended?" said Patrick.

Mr Grant frowned. "Well, perhaps it could have been" – he glanced towards his workbench – "soldered, perhaps." He looked back at Patrick. "Tell, you what. Go out and look by the front gate, near the bins. It might still be there." He glanced towards the house. "I'd go myself, but . . ."

Patrick understood. He turned and stepped out of the shed.

He sniffed the air. It smelled as if someone was having a bonfire.

As he walked up towards the house, something made Patrick glance at the kitchen window. Was something moving in there? Or was it his imagination? What *was* it?

The smell of burning seemed to be getting stronger. Patrick quickened his step – and *wow!* Now he could see grey smoke pouring out of the top of the kitchen window!

Patrick started to run.

In seconds he was peering into the Grants' kitchen. What a terrible sight! There were flames – huge leaping flames that broke from the cooker and climbed higher and higher towards the ceiling.

Whoosh! Suddenly the flames were nearly hidden in a billow of smoke.

He heard a gasp. It was his own.

The house was on fire – and his friends were in there!

For a split second he wondered what to do.

The next minute he was running – running as fast as his legs would take him.

Uncle Dickie was just pulling something out of a top hat, when Patrick burst into the room.

The smirk vanished and his mouth fell open, as Patrick, with all the power of his lungs, yelled, "FIRE!"

Eleven

Things move very quickly when you shout "Fire!"

Things moved very quickly when Patrick shouted "Fire!"

Mrs Grant got everyone into the garden in seconds. (The passage was quite safe, though there was a horrible smell of burning.)

Uncle Dickie dialled 999 on his mobile phone, and suddenly seemed quite normal.

"Wow! This is the best party ever!" Tamsin cried, as everyone crowded round the kitchen window to watch the firemen put out the fire. It didn't take them long.

The cupboard beside the cooker was badly burnt, and some of the other units were blackened. But otherwise there wasn't much damage.

The firemen soon worked out how the fire had started. It was Mrs Grant's fault. She had put the grill on rather than the oven for the sausages, then flung the oven gloves over the grill while it was still on. The oven gloves had slowly caught fire, and then set fire to the cupboard.

"It was so stupid of me!" Mrs Grant said ruefully.

"Well, you were fussed over my party," said Sophie.

Mrs Grant squeezed Sophie's hand, and smiled at Patrick. "Thank goodness you spotted it, and raised the alarm!"

Half an hour later she was saying the same thing to Patrick's mum, who had come to collect him. "Patrick was brilliant! It could have been so much worse!"

"We could have been frizzled!" cried Tamsin.

"We could have been frazzled!" cried Sophie.

"We could have been sizzled!" cried Tamsin.

"But we weren't!" said Sophie.

Mum looked bewildered. "But . . . but how . . . ?"

Mrs Grant explained about the sausages and the grill. "It was so daft of me. But Patrick raised the alarm before the fire did serious damage." She gave a little sigh. "Thank goodness he was in the garden . . ."

There was a pause.

Then Mum said, "In the *garden*?"

"Yes," said Sophie.

"While everyone else was in the house?"

"Yes," said Tamsin.

"We were all watching Uncle Dickie," said Sophie.

"Uncle Dickie and me," said Tamsin.

Mum turned to Patrick. "Patrick?"

"Yes?"

"What were you *doing* in the garden?"

There was silence. Everyone was looking at him.

Patrick cleared his throat.

And then—

"Why shouldn't he be in the garden?"

Twelve

Everyone swung round.

Mr Grant was standing by the door to the kitchen. He seemed different somehow, thought Patrick. More confident . . .

"Daddy!" cried Sophie, running to him.

Mr Grant put an arm round her, then turned to Mum. "He was most welcome in the garden. Really."

Mum frowned. "But the party was in the house!"

There was silence.

"But Patrick doesn't like parties," said Tamsin.

"Not even mine," said Sophie sadly.

"I don't understand it," said Tamsin.

"But there it is," said Sophie.

"It's one of those things," said Tamsin.

"We're all different," said Sophie.

Suddenly Mum gave a sigh. "No. He doesn't like parties . . ."

"Some people don't," said Mr Grant.

Mum looked at Patrick. "It's his birthday next month too. I don't know what I'm going to do about that."

Patrick looked at Mr Grant.

Mr Grant looked at Patrick.

"Patrick?" said Mr Grant.

"Yes?"

"What would you like to do on your birthday?"

Patrick thought. "What – anything?"

"Anything."

"Hmmm." Suddenly Patrick thought of Mr Grant's workbench. "I'd like to make something."

Mr Grant smiled. "You mean, woodwork?"

"Yes."

"Woodwork! Yeuch!" cried Sophie.

"The sawdust gets up my nose!"

Mr Grant took no notice. "Would you like to do it with a friend?"

Patrick thought again. "Yes. With Luke."

"Luke is his friend," Tamsin explained.

"Excellent!" said Mr Grant. "I'll get some stuff in the shed, and sharpen my tools." His eyes brightened. "I haven't done any carpentry for ages!" He turned to Mum. "Are you happy about this?"

Mum frowned. "Well, it doesn't seem . . ."

Mr Grant smiled. "And then I'll take everyone out to dinner. It's the least I can do after Patrick saved our kitchen."

"Well . . ." said Mum.

Mr Grant's eyes narrowed thoughtfully. "In fact I'll take you to my favourite restaurant."

Sophie gasped. "Say yes!" she hissed to Mum.

Mrs Grant was smiling.

Everyone was looking at Mum.

What was she going to say?

Mum looked at Patrick. "Would you really like to do that on your birthday, Patrick?"

"Yes," said Patrick.

There was another silence.

And then – suddenly – Mum laughed. "Thank you!" she said to Mr Grant. "That would be lovely!"

Thirteen

Patrick had a wonderful birthday.

Mr Grant turned out to be a very good carpenter (though surprisingly strict on the safety front).

Patrick wanted to make a digger at first (the metal one was never found), but Mr Grant persuaded him it was too difficult.

Instead he made a tool box out of pine-wood.

Luke made a toilet-roll holder.

Both items were much admired.

Sophie kept on bringing snacks down to the shed, until Mr Grant told her to stop, because no one would be hungry for dinner.

After the carpenters had tidied the shed and got changed, Mr Grant took everyone out to his favourite restaurant. There were seven people altogether – Mr Grant, Mrs Grant, Mum, Patrick, Luke, Sophie and (for some reason) Tamsin.

Everyone said they could see why it was Mr Grant's favourite restaurant – even Luke, who really only liked burger bars.

Mum loved it.

She said it was "as good as a holiday!" and spent a long time talking to Mr Grant about his books.

Mum was still smiling when she and Patrick got back to the flat.

"Wasn't that a lovely evening?" she said, kicking her shoes off.

"Yes."

"Such fun!"

Patrick carried his tool box over to the table, and set it down. He stood back to admire it once again.

Then he looked at his marble run.

He was pleased with Marble Run City.

It looked good.

It looked very good.

Patrick picked up a marble.

"So generous of Andrew!" said Mum, collapsing into a chair.

"Very."

"Seven of us – you can't say that wasn't a party!"

"No."

Patrick rolled his marble round his hand.

Mum laughed. "You and parties – I don't know!"

"I don't know either."

"What do you mean?"

Patrick dropped the marble down the chute at the top of Marble Run City. A clatter – and it was off. "Well, I'll never like parties, not really. But I don't think I have such a problem with them now." He could hear the marble gathering speed.

Mum looked at him closely. "You don't?"

"No."

The marble made it past a tricky edge, where it sometimes got stuck, and started whooshing down a long straight.

"But why the change? What happened?"

"What happened?" He looked at her. "I met another – that's what happened."

Now the marble had passed a dangerous corner, and was on the home run.

"Met another?" said Mum. "Another what?"

Patrick thought back to that day.

The day of Sophie's party.

The day he realized he was not alone after all.

And he grinned.

"I met another party-hater . . ."

The marble finished its run – and flew out free into the room.

ASTRID, THE AU PAIR FROM OUTER SPACE

Emily Smith

Imagine being looked after by an alien from outer space…

When Harry's mum says they're getting an 'au pair' from another country, he's not quite sure what to expect. When Astrid, who lives on a planet 500 light years away, decides to work as an 'au pair' on Earth, she's not quite sure what to expect.

What Harry definitely doesn't expect is a girl whose suitcase moves on its own. And Astrid is very surprised to find that Harry's family has a special gadget for opening tins and that his little brother Fred isn't a girl!

SMARTIES SILVER MEDAL WINNER

ISBN 0552 54616X

THE SHRIMP

Emily Smith

Wild life!

Ben spends the holidays with his nose in the sand and bottom in the air. It's not because he's shy – though some of his classmates do call him the Shrimp. It's because he's got a great idea for his wildlife project.

A competition is on! The class projects are going to be judged by a famous TV wildlife presenter, and the prize is irresistible. Ben would love to win it, but others have their eyes on the prize too...

SMARTIES GOLD MEDAL WINNER

ISBN 0552 547352

ROBOMUM

Emily Smith

"A robot mother?
Is that what you want?
A Robomum?"

James's mum is a brilliant scientist, but James wishes she was better at the ordinary things in life. He'd really like to have a clean PE kit, interesting food for tea and the films that he wants on video, but Mum's got other things on her mind. Then, in a flash of inspiration, Mum realizes how to improve the situation. Surely a robotic mother – a Robomum – is just what they both need?

A highly entertaining story by an award-winning author that will be loved by young readers – and their mothers!

ISBN 0552 547360